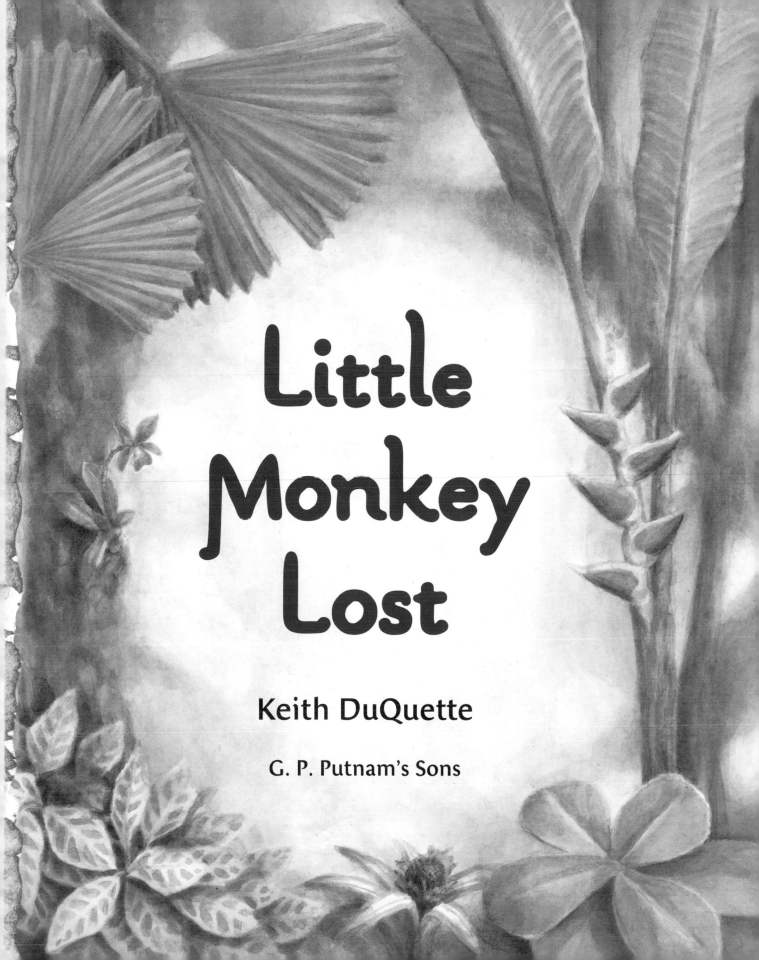

Little Monkey Lost

Keith DuQuette

G. P. Putnam's Sons

In the deepest jungle there lived a troop
of monkeys. Every day was just the same.
They lounged in the trees, munched on leaves,
and took long naps.

Little Monkey
was *sooo* bored!

One morning, while the rest of his troop was sleeping, he saw a lily pad float by.

"I'll take a ride," he said to himself. "Now, that will be fun!"

Just then his mother woke up. "Little Monkey, come back!" she shouted.

But in no time Little Monkey was far, far from home.

This part of the jungle was a little scary. Little Monkey wanted to go home.

Then, he remembered what his mother once told him: "If you ever get lost, find other monkeys. They will lead you home."

But these creatures didn't look like monkeys!

Little Monkey climbed farther up the tree. There he met some animals that were making a racket. They looked like they might be monkeys!

"Excuse me," Little Monkey asked. "Are you monkeys?"

"THAT'S RIGHT," they hollered.

"COME HOOWWWLL WITH US!"

"Hooooooooowwwoooowwwwllll," he shouted. It felt so good to let it out!

After a while, Little Monkey asked them how to get home. But they wouldn't stop howling!

Suddenly, he saw a fast-moving group. They definitely looked like monkeys.

"Hey! Wait," Little Monkey shouted. "Are you guys monkeys?"

"You bet we are," they answered. "Come swing with us!"

Little Monkey had never moved like
this before. He felt so free!
But after a while, his arms began to ache.
He stopped to rest on a branch.

There he came upon two furry creatures with long tails like his.

"Are you two monkeys?" Little Monkey asked.

"We certainly are," they said. "Come hug with us."

"Well, okay, I guess." Little Monkey didn't want to be rude.

He loved the warm feeling of the hug. But this hug went on forever!

Finally, Little Monkey wriggled away.

That afternoon, Little Monkey met many other kinds of monkeys.

They all showed him something different, but nobody knew the way home.

Little Monkey had never had such a busy day.
And he had never been so sleepy . . .

It was the middle of the night when Little Monkey woke up. He was surrounded by eight enormous eyes!

"Are you monkeys?" Little Monkey bravely asked.

"Yes, we are," they said. "Come eat with us."

Little Monkey had not eaten a single leaf all day!

"Try this," the smallest monkey said.

The heavy fruit was sweet and juicy. It was the best thing Little Monkey had ever eaten.

Little Monkey played all night
with the big-eyed monkeys.

The next morning,
they disappeared into
the trees. Little Monkey
was all alone.

He took a deep breath and howled.
"Maamaaa, where are yooooouuuuu?"

Way off in the distance, he
heard a voice call back!
Little Monkey swung from
branch to branch to follow the
far-off voice. And though his tiny
arms ached, he kept swinging . . .

. . . until just around a tree he finally saw his troop!
They were all wide-awake and so happy to see him.
"Little Monkey, Little Monkey, you're home,"
his mother said. "We were so worried about you!"

"I'm sorry. I just wanted to have some fun. I didn't mean to get lost," said Little Monkey. "But I got to play with lots of monkeys, and they showed me so many things to do!"

Little Monkey's mother frowned. "Like what?" she asked.

"They taught me to howl," Little Monkey said, "and to swing from branch to branch, and to eat delicious fruits, and to hug. Like this."
Finally, Little Monkey's mother smiled.

And from that day forward,
Little Monkey was never bored again—
and neither was his troop.

Meet the Monkeys

All of the monkeys featured in this book are New World monkeys. They live in the lush jungles of South and Central America.

Squirrel Monkey

Little Monkey and his troop are squirrel monkeys. These very vocal, agile, and inquisitive monkeys often share their territories with capuchin monkeys, where there are more eyes and ears to watch out for jungle predators, like the harpy eagles and large snakes.

Howler Monkey

These large, slow-moving monkeys are some of the loudest animals to live on earth. Their booming calls mark out their territory to other monkey troops. They can be heard in the jungle as far as two miles away.

Night Monkey

The only New World monkeys that are active at night. They spend their days sleeping in tree hollows and tangles of vine. Their enormous owl-like eyes are perfectly adapted to life in the jungle night. That is why they are also called owl monkeys.

Tamarin

Wild hair seems to be a feature of all the species of these small monkeys. Tamarins usually give birth to twins. Both the mother and father raise their young. The three species shown here are the golden lion, emperor, and cotton-top tamarins.

Spider Monkey

A dynamic, athletic monkey that moves through the jungle in five-limbed flight—two arms, two legs, and a remarkable prehensile, or grabbing, tail.

Titi Monkey

When resting, grooming, or sleeping, these small monkeys can be found hugging one another with tails entwined. Males and females mate for life and live in small family groups. Most of the time, the father carries the baby after it is born.

Uakari

A rare and unusual species. Male uakaris' (wah-CAR-ees) scarlet red faces are known to brighten when they are excited or angry. Though they do not have long grasping tails like howler and spider monkeys, uakaris are expert climbers.

Marmoset

The quiet pygmy marmoset is the smallest of the New World monkeys. Like most monkeys it eats fruit and insects, but it also spends much of its time clinging to trees, feeding on tree saps and gums.

Capuchin

Considered the most intelligent of all New World species, capuchins have been observed cracking open nuts by smashing them with stones or by banging the nut on hard surfaces.

To Virginia

Special thanks to the
Brooklyn Botanic Garden.
A jungle grows in Brooklyn—
who woulda thunk it?

G. P. PUTNAM'S SONS
A division of Penguin Young Readers Group.
Published by The Penguin Group.
Penguin Group (USA) Inc.,
375 Hudson Street, New York, NY 10014, U.S.A.
Penguin Group (Canada), 90 Eglinton Avenue East,
Suite 700, Toronto, Ontario, Canada M4P 2Y3
(a division of Pearson Penguin Canada Inc.).
Penguin Books Ltd, 80 Strand, London WC2R 0RL, England.
Penguin Ireland, 25 St. Stephen's Green, Dublin 2, Ireland
(a division of Penguin Books Ltd.).
Penguin Group (Australia), 250 Camberwell Road, Camberwell, Victoria 3124, Australia
(a division of Pearson Australia Group Pty Ltd).
Penguin Books India Pvt Ltd, 11 Community Centre, Panchsheel Park, New Delhi - 110 017, India.
Penguin Group (NZ), Cnr Airborne and Rosedale Roads, Albany, Auckland 1310, New Zealand
(a division of Pearson New Zealand Ltd).
Penguin Books (South Africa) (Pty) Ltd, 24 Sturdee Avenue, Rosebank, Johannesburg 2196, South Africa.
Penguin Books Ltd, Registered Offices: 80 Strand, London WC2R 0RL, England.

Published simultaneously in Canada. Manufactured in China by South China Printing Co. Ltd.
Design by Katrina Damkoehler. Text set in Bebop Medium.

Library of Congress Cataloging-in-Publication Data
Du Quette, Keith. Little Monkey lost / by Keith DuQuette.   p. cm.
Summary: Bored, Little Monkey sets out to find adventure in the jungle and meets nine different kinds of monkeys
who teach him fun new things, but not how to get home. Includes facts about the New World Monkeys featured.
[1. Monkeys—Fiction. 2. Jungles—Fiction. 3. Lost children—Fiction.] I. Title.
PZ7.C187Lit 2007   [E]—dc22   2006013252

ISBN 978-0-399-24294-6
1 2 3 4 5 6 7 8 9 10
First Impression